ROMANTASY
COLORING BOOK

chartwell
books

Create Your Happily Ever After!

Step beyond the ordinary into a magical world. There are mystical creatures–fairies and unicorns–and there are dangers–dragons and gargoyles. But you are not afraid. You're the hero of this story. And *this* story always has a happy ending!

Romantasy Coloring Book lets you live out your dreams in a place where love conquers all. Handsome knights in shining armor, stolen kisses in the moonlight: they're all here for you to color into life. Let your creative side take you on flights of fancy. There's no greater force in the world than love! As you choose your colors, you're inventing your own unforgettable romance.

You'll fall for all the beautiful images in this book, imagining the stories that surround them. Whether you visualize an all-important, high-stakes quest or you picture the figures on the page vanquishing foes at the gate of a castle, you're in charge of this story. Pick up the media of your choice and settle in before bed, during a break from work, or any time you just need a few moments of escape.

You don't have to have artistic talent to enjoy this coloring book. Leave the real world behind and enter a place where true love and passion rule. Start dreaming!

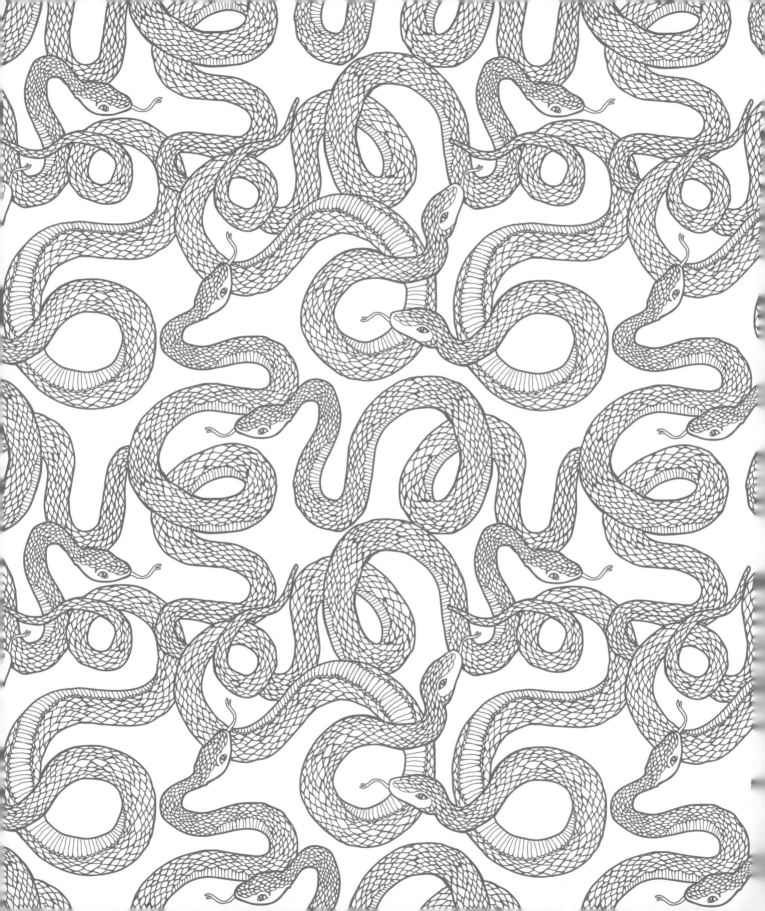

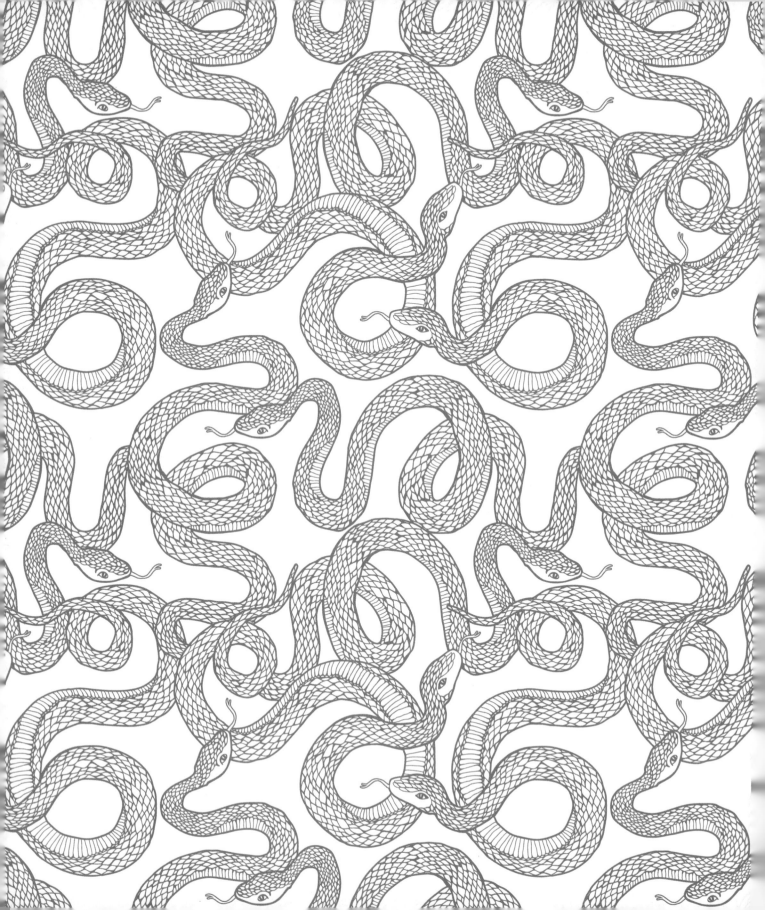

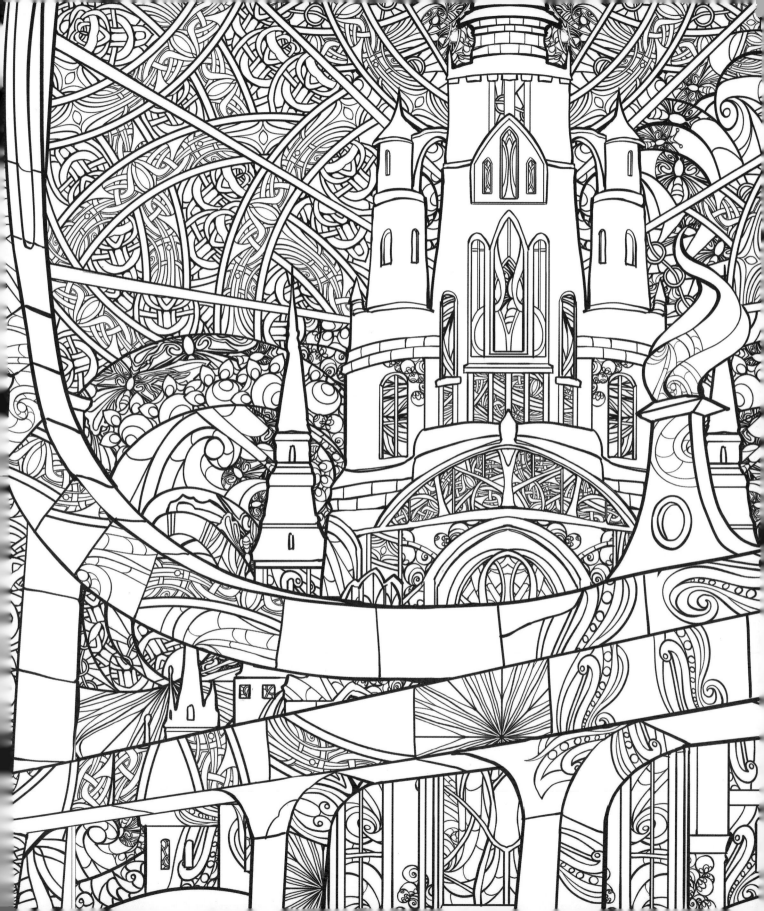

Quarto

This edition published in 2024 by Chartwell Books,
an imprint of The Quarto Group
142 West 36th Street, 4th Floor
New York, NY 10018 USA
T (212) 779-4972 F (212) 779-6058
www.Quarto.com

10 9 8 7 6 5 4 3 2 1

Chartwell titles are also available at discount for retail, wholesale, promotional, and bulk purchase. For details, contact the Special Sales Manager by email at special-sales@quarto.com or by mail at The Quarto Group, Attn: Special Sales Manager, 100 Cummings Center Suite 265D, Beverly, MA 01915, USA.

ISBN: 978-0-7858-4533-1

Publisher: Wendy Friedman
Senior Publishing Director: Meredith Mennitt
Designers: Sue Boylan and Alana Ward
Editor: Joanne O'Sullivan
Image credits: Shutterstock

Printed in China